And then he cleaned his rugby boots.

But being Mr Strong he polished his boots so hard that he wore them down to nothing!

Luckily he had a spare pair.

MR. MEN
THE RUGBY MATCH

Roger Hargreaves

Original concept by
Roger Hargreaves

Written and illustrated by
Adam Hargreaves

EGMONT

Mr Strong was very excited. He was going to play in the biggest rugby game of his life.

He was the captain.

It was his rugby team. And they were going to play the best side in the world.

The All Reds.

Who had never lost a game.

He got up very early and had breakfast.

Lots of eggs to keep him strong.

Then he tested the match ball.

He squeezed it to see if there was enough air in it.

BANG!

He had popped the ball.

Mr Strong really does not know his own strength!

Luckily he had a spare ball.

It was a very proud moment for Mr Strong when he stepped out onto the pitch.

But Mr Strong was also a bit nervous.

Would the team that he had chosen live up to the challenge?

And when the mighty All Reds came onto the pitch Mr Strong felt even more nervous.

But not as nervous as Mr Jelly.

He took one look at the All Reds.

And ran.

All the way back to the changing room!

The game got under way.

Mr Forgetful kicked off.

Well, not so much kicked off as teed off.

Mr Forgetful had forgotten what game he was playing!

For a while Mr Strong's team did surprisingly well.

Mr Tickle's extraordinarily long arms proved to be very useful for tackling.

He tackled here.

And he tackled there.

He tackled all over the pitch.

The All Reds could not get past him.

Mr Greedy was like a one man scrum.

In fact he was a one man scrum.

He was so heavy the All Reds could not move him one inch.

And then, wonder of wonders, Mr Strong's team scored a try.

The ball had been passed to Mr Rush who raced down the wing to score.

What a try!

Mr Strong began to think they might have a chance of winning.

But after scoring the try Mr Rush just kept
on running ...

And Mr Fussy decided he did not like all the mud and retired to the changing room for a bath ...

And Mr Bounce got mistaken for the ball and kicked out of the ground.

Mr Strong was losing players as fast as …

… well, as fast as Mr Rush had left the pitch.

The All Reds then scored a try as quickly as Mr Muddle had muddled up which team he was playing for.

Nice pass Mr Muddle!

Mr Strong realised it was going to take a miracle to win the game.

There was only a minute left to play.

However, when you have Mr Impossible on your team miracles are never impossible.

Mr Impossible's flying try was exactly that!

And then the final whistle was blown.

Mr Strong could hardly believe it.

His team had won!

They had won against the mighty All Reds.

And the All Reds?

The All Reds were very embarrassed.

They had never lost a game.

You might say they were all red in the face!